MONSTAR'S
Messy School Day

There are lots of Early Reader
stories you might enjoy.

Look at the back of the book or,
for a complete list, visit
www.orionchildrensbooks.co.uk

MONSTAR'S
Messy School Day

STEVE COLE
Illustrated by PETE WILLIAMSON

Orion
Children's Books

ORION CHILDREN'S BOOKS

First published in Great Britain in 2017
by Hodder and Stoughton

1 3 5 7 9 10 8 6 4 2

Text © Steve Cole, 2017
Illustrations © Pete Williamson, 2017

A CIP catalogue record for this book
is available from the British Library.

ISBN 978 1 4440 1465 5

Printed and bound in China

The paper and board used in this book are from well-managed forests
and other responsible sources.

MIX
Paper from
responsible sources
FSC® C104740

Orion Children's Books
An imprint of
Hachette Children's Group
Part of Hodder and Stoughton
Carmelite House
50 Victoria Embankment
London EC4Y 0DZ

An Hachette UK Company
www.hachette.co.uk

www.hachettechildrens.co.uk

For Harriet and Jemima

Contents

Chapter One

Jen and Jon's parents were crazy inventors.

One day they invented a special monster pet.

Her fur grew in the shape of a star over one eye.

That is why Jen and Jon
named her . . .
MONSTAR.

Monstar was fun. She was kind.

And she was very good at
making a mess!

Mum and Dad did not like messes.
"Monstar!" Mum shouted. "Stop
digging holes in the hall carpet!"

"Monstar!" cried Dad. "Don't
wear muddy wellies on the sofa!"

Monstar went to her bed in a sulk. "Me always messing up."

Chapter Two

When Jen got in from school that day, she gave her pet a cuddle. "Monstar can't help being messy!"

"She just gets bored when we're at school," said Jon.

"Me wish ME could go to school," mumbled Monstar.

That night, Monstar overheard
Mum and Dad talking about her.
She sneaked out of bed to listen.

"Let's send Monstar to that class tomorrow," said Mum.

"The sooner the better," Dad agreed. "She needs a good teacher."

"Teacher? Class?" Monstar jumped up in delight. "Ooooh! Me going to SCHOOL!"

Monstar was so excited she couldn't sleep for AGES.

Chapter Three

The next day, at half-past eight, Jen and Jon went off to school.

The front door swung shut behind them.
SLAM!

Monstar woke up – and gasped.
"Me late for school!"
She rushed to the bathroom to
wash her face and paws.

She tied her prettiest bows on her horns and took Jen's spare uniform. She packed a bag with pencils and paper.

But what about food? Jen and Jon always took a packed lunch. Monstar took Mum's new invention – a magic bowl that never overflowed – and poured in piles of green porridge.

Then she ran to school.
All the children were inside
when Monstar arrived.

"Hey, you!" someone called.
"You're late."

It was the Head Teacher!

Chapter Four

The Head peered down at
Monstar. What an unusual child!
she thought.

"Are you in Class One?"

Monstar gulped. "Er . . . maybe."

"I'll take you there," said the Head.

The children in Class One were painting pictures.

Their teacher smiled at Monstar and gave her some paintbrushes. "Would you like to paint a picture?"

"Me love painting!" Monstar
jumped onto the nearest table.
  But she didn't paint with brushes.
She used her tail!

"Much easier!" said Monstar.
But it was also much messier . . .
"Oops!"

"Oops, indeed." The teacher wiped yellow paint from his eye. "I think you should try a different class!"

Chapter Five

Monstar was taken to Class Two.
The children were sitting quietly
at their tables.

"We are all reading books." The teacher smiled. "Choose one from the box."

"Ooooh!" Monstar was excited. "Me love books!" She couldn't read words very well but she loved to look at pictures. Especially cute animal pictures.

Which book should she choose? She flicked through the first book box but couldn't find anything she liked.

She searched the second book box. Nothing there either!
She looked through the third book box … and the fourth …

"Oh, dear me!" The teacher
brushed books off her head.
"You've made such a mess!"
"Oops!" said Monstar.

Chapter Six

The bell went for lunch time. Monstar followed the other children to the dinner hall.

She licked her lips. The special
magic bowl she'd packed was
FULL of green porridge!

But some had slopped out. It was very sticky. The bowl was stuck inside her bag.

Monstar pulled at the bowl.
She wobbled it.
She shook it.

"Come out!" Monstar grabbed the gooey bowl and heaved. "Come… OUT!"

With a final, furious tug, the bowl did come out.

Green porridge went EVERYWHERE.

SPLAT! It soaked the children on the next table.

SLOOSH! It sloshed over the dinner ladies.

SPLOSH! It splashed the teachers on their table.

Soon, pupils and were slipping
and sliding through a big green
porridge-puddle all over the floor.
CLANG! They slid into tables.
BANG! They whumped into walls.

"Monstar!" Jen and Jon slid through the slimy porridge to give their pet a hug. "What are YOU doing here?"

The Head splashed up to them.
"Do you know this pupil?"
  "She's our pet," said Jon.
"Monstar."

"Pet?" The Head was so shocked she fell over on her bottom with a SQUELCH. "We can't have pets in school. Monstar has got to go!"

Chapter Seven

Mum and Dad came to take
Monstar and the magic bowl back
home.

"You made a mistake, Monstar," said Mum. "When we said we would send you to a class, we meant an *obedience* class!"

"At Monster Training School," Dad added.

"Monster Training School?" Monstar grinned. "Me likes the sound of that!"

So, that evening, Mum and Dad and Jen and Jon took Monstar to Monster Training School.

A purple monster opened the door. He was holding a large orange jelly. "Aha! This must be Monstar, here for some lessons. Do come in."

"I say!" said Dad. "It's a bit messy and mucky around here."

"Yes," said the purple monster. "Isn't it lovely?"

"But . . ." Mum frowned. "We thought you would teach Monstar to be neat and smart."

"No way!" the purple monster cried. "At Monster Training School, we teach monsters how to be EVEN MORE monster-y. And monsters LOVE making mess!"

He pushed the orange jelly into
Monstar's face!
"See?!"

Monstar laughed. Then she threw jelly back at the teacher. The teacher ducked, and the jelly hit Mum and Dad instead!

"This is yucky!" wailed Dad.
"It's mucky!" Mum moaned.

"It's FUN!" Monstar gave Jen and Jon a big, sticky hug.

"Messy school days are the best – and this will be messiest one EVER!"